For Rafe and his buddies Isaac and Auggie

MB

To Santa

JK

# HOW DOES SANTA GO DOWN THE CHIMNEY?

by Mac Barnett
illustrated by Jon Klassen

CANDLEWICK PRESS

How does he do it?

How does it work?

Does he cinch up his belt?

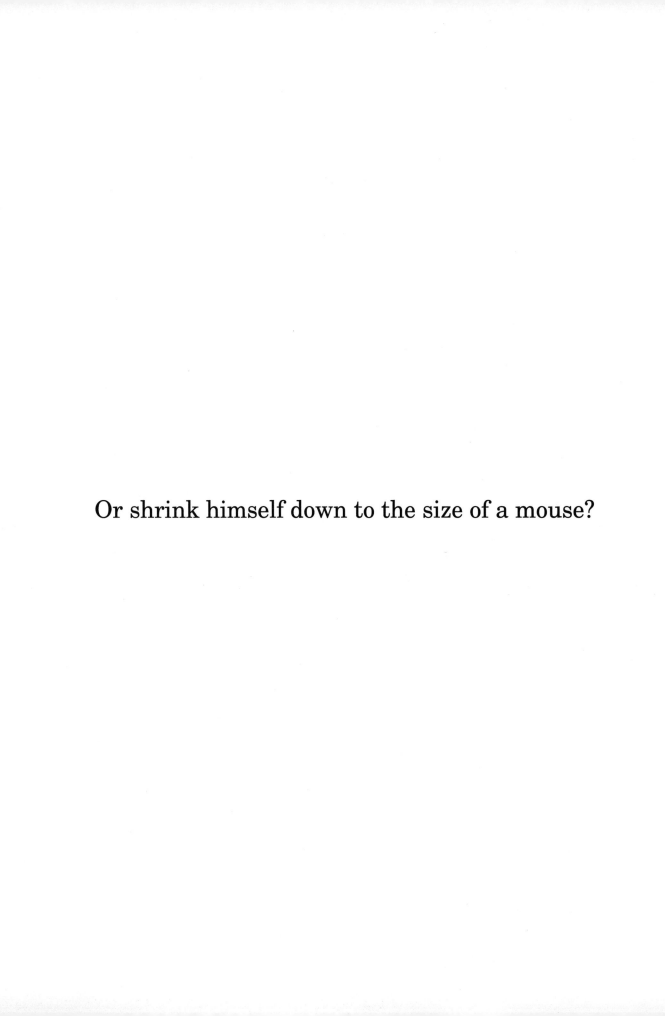

Or shrink himself down to the size of a mouse?

Or
stretch
out
like
taffy
and
step
in
one
leg
at
a
time?

Maybe
Santa
can
turn
into
fire!

But
probably
not.

Does
he go
headfirst?

Or
feetfirst?

Or
neither?

Does Santa ever get stuck partway down
and need one of the reindeer to give him a kick?

Does his suit get real sooty?

Because chimneys have soot.

And then does Santa do laundry
before he goes to the next house?

And if you don't have a chimney,

what happens then?

Maybe Santa knows about
the key under the flowerpot,
even though nobody is ever,
*ever*
supposed to mention
the key under the flowerpot.

So how would he find out about that?

Does he flatten himself and slide under your door?

Or does he slip through the pipes
and come out of your faucet?

If you've got a mail slot,
I bet Santa folds up like a letter
and has a reindeer pop him through.
And I bet the stamp on Santa
is one of those Santa stamps too.

Dogs must like Santa very much, or else they'd bark.
He probably carries treats in his pocket and knows
just where every dog likes to be scratched.

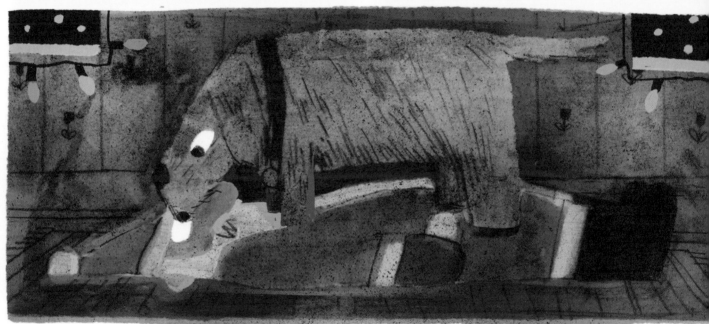

He tells them they're good, and whispers their names,
which he knows without even looking at their collars.
I bet he lets them give him kisses, right on his beard,
if they're the kind of dogs that like to lick.

Can Santa see in the dark? Does he wear night-vision goggles that make everything green? I bet he'd like that. Because Santa likes green.

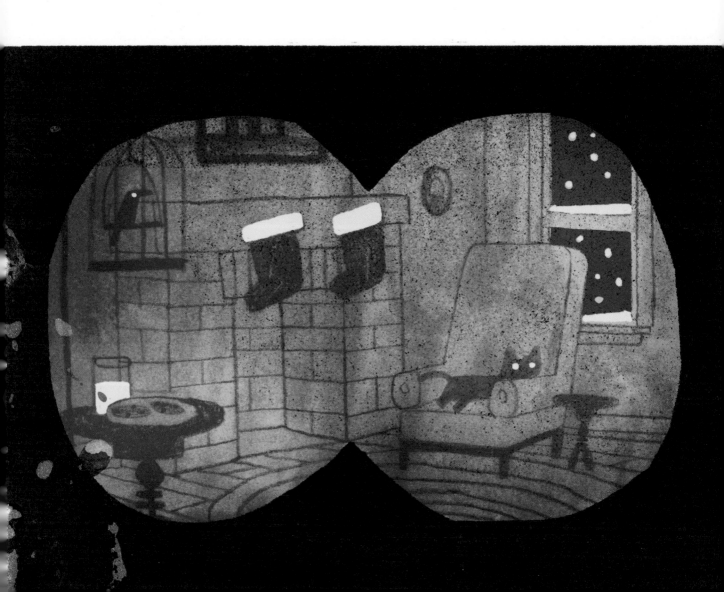

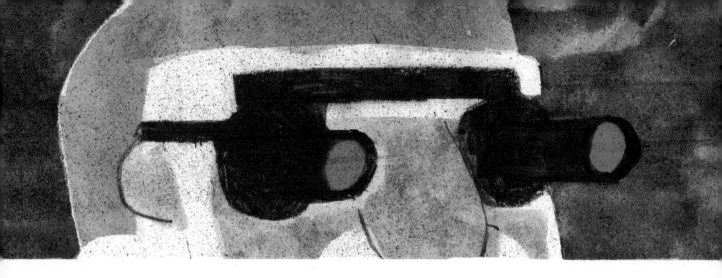

Or heat-vision goggles?

Because he might like red better.

Should we leave out carrots, not cookies, on Christmas Eve, since they're good for his eyesight?

No. The twinkling lights on the tree
will make enough light for Santa to see,
tiptoeing past chairs without bumping his knee

to leave a present, or two, or three,
and get a kiss from the dog (if it's a dog that licks),
and take a cookie, or two, or three, and then leave.

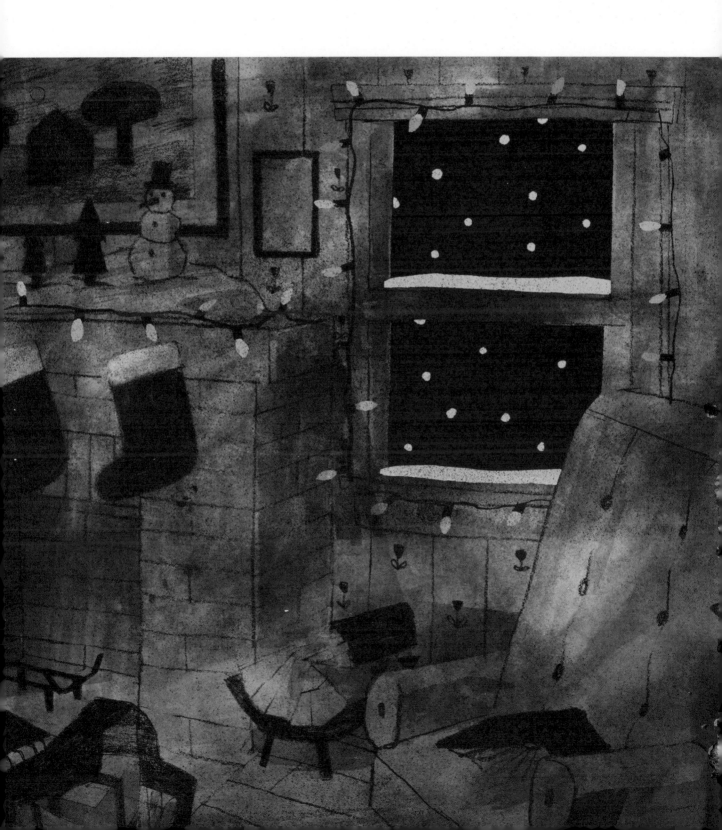

Santa goes up the chimney the same way he comes down.

And I have no idea how Santa does that.

But I'm so glad he can.